# Brian Wildsmith
# The Nest

## Oxford University Press

Oxford  Toronto  Melbourne

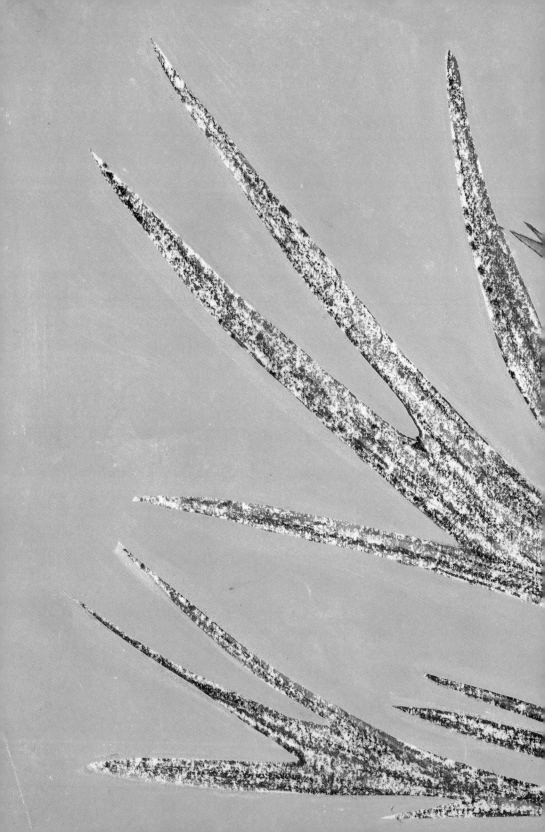

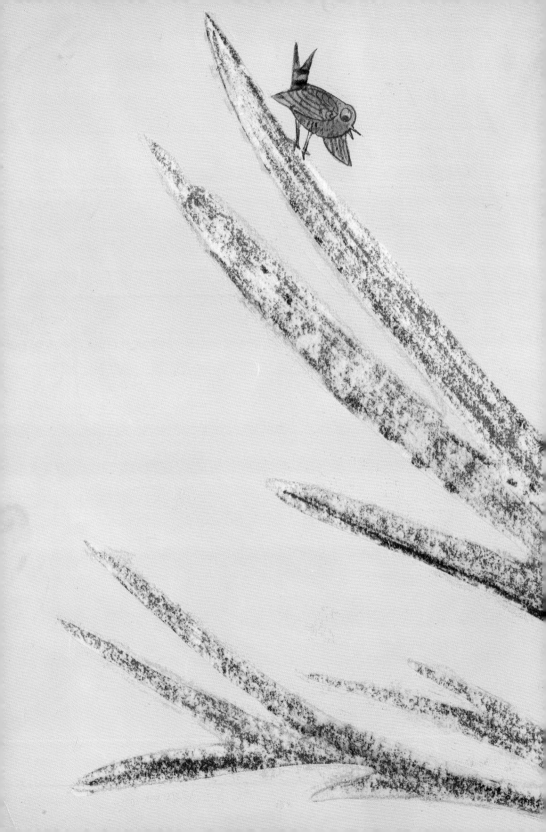

Oxford University Press, Walton Street, Oxford OX2 6DP

Oxford   New York
Athens   Auckland   Bangkok   Bombay
Calcutta   Cape Town   Dar es Salaam   Delhi
Florence   Hong Kong   Istanbul   Karachi
Kuala Lumpur   Madras   Madrid   Melbourne
Mexico City   Nairobi   Paris   Singapore
Taipei   Tokyo   Toronto

and associated companies in
Berlin   Ibadan

Oxford is a trade mark of Oxford University Press

This edition is also available in
Oxford Reading Tree Branch Library Stage 1 Pack **A**
**ISBN 0 19 272100 3**

British Library Cataloguing in Publication Data
Wildsmith, Brian
The nest.
I.   Title
823'.914[J]   PZ7
ISBN 0-19-272134-8

Printed in Hong Kong